Dear Friend,
Dear Reader,
Look at the book
you have just opened.
What is it
you hold in your hand?

Friend,
ar Reader,
t the book

O K

by George Ella Lyon
paintings by Peter Catalanotto

A DK INK BOOK
DK PUBLISHING, INC.

For Dick and Peter,
for Ann,
and for all at Community Montessori
who make it such a wonderful place to grow
—G.E.L.

For Miss Dunn,
Dick Jackson,
and the man in the boat
—P.C.

Special thanks to Tory
—P.C.

A Richard Jackson Book

DK
Ink

DK Publishing, Inc.
95 Madison Avenue
New York, New York 10016

Visit us on the World Wide Web at http://www.dk.com

Library of Congress Cataloging-in-Publication Data
Lyon, George Ella [date]
Book / by George Ella Lyon; paintings by Peter Catalanotto.—1st ed.
p.   cm.
"A Richard Jackson book."
Summary: This poem compares a book to a house, a treasure chest, a farm,
and a tree full of leaves.
ISBN 0-7894-2560-2
1. Books and reading—Juvenile poetry.   2. Children's poetry, American.
[1. Books and reading—Poetry.   2. American poetry.]
I. Catalanotto, Peter, ill.   II. Title.
PS3562.Y4454B66   1999   811'.54—dc21   98-19835   CIP   AC

The illustrations for this book were painted in watercolor.
The text of this book is set in 22 point Goudy Catalogue.
Book design by Liney Li
Printed and bound in U.S.A.

First Edition, 1999
10 9 8 7 6 5 4 3 2 1

A BOOK is a HOUSE
that is all windows and doors.

Some walls are slick
with the zing of ink,
some old and cloth-soft,
smelling of dust.

Walk in.
Find your way.
Light falls
through the windows of words.

fields so

Learn the secret

A BO K is a CHEST

find your way

or a child

a cave

L ft the

castle

po

heart treasure

in lid **BOOK**

look in

Lea
Field
passage

ny

A BOOK is

Learn the secret
passages.

Turn

pages, corners,
holding your breath.

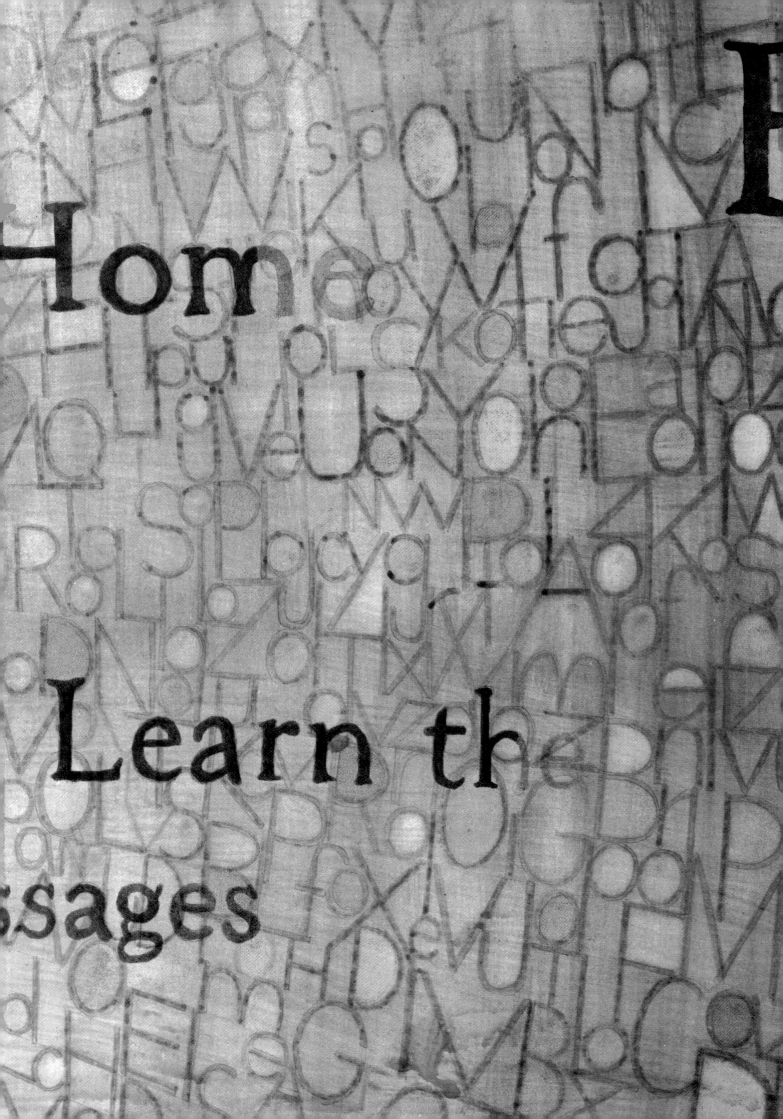

A BOOK is a CHEST
that keeps the heart's treasure.
Lift the plain lid
and look in.

You may find a castle,
a cave,
a wild pony,

or a child
in a farmhouse,
opening a chest.

Heart's treasure

A BOOK is a FARM,
its fields sown with words.

Reader, you are its weather:
your tears, your eyes shining.
The writer, working these words,
cried and laughed, too.

Now you meet

as the gate of the book
swings wide.

Dear Friend, Dear Reader,

A BOOK is full of LEAVES
that feed the tree of life,
each page
bound on one edge,
free on three.

BOOK   BOON COMPANION

Field

Home

Treasure

May it hold you.
May it set you free.